Mildred D. Taylor

THE WELL
DAVID'S STORY

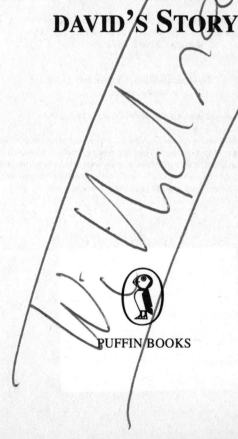

PUFFIN BOOKS

PUFFIN BOOKS

Published by the Penguin Group
Penguin Books Ltd, 27 Wrights Lane, London W8 5TZ, England
Penguin Books USA Inc., 375 Hudson Street, New York, New York 10014, USA
Penguin Books Australia Ltd, Ringwood, Victoria, Australia
Penguin Books Canada Ltd, 10 Alcorn Avenue, Toronto, Ontario, Canada M4V 3B2
Penguin Books (NZ) Ltd, 182–190 Wairau Road, Auckland 10, New Zealand

Penguin Books Ltd, Registered Offices: Harmondsworth, Middlesex, England

First published in the USA by Dial Books for Young Readers 1995
First published in Great Britain by Victor Gollancz Ltd 1995
Published in Puffin Books 1997
1 3 5 7 9 10 8 6 4 2

This book is dedicated
to the memory of my beloved father,
the storyteller,
and
to my mother, my sister, all my family,
past and present,
who have always been there for me,
and
to my beautiful, exquisite daughter,
P. Laurén
who has enlightened my life.

Author's Note

When I was a child, my family always told stories about the past—stories about parents, grandparents, greatgrandparents, stories about aunts and uncles and cousins, neighbours and friends, stories about the young and the old, stories about themselves. They were stories that reached back into time, some even into slavery. Wherever the family gathered, in our northern home where I grew up or in the South where I was born, the stories were told. Some of the stories were humorous, some were tragic, but all taught me a history not then written in textbooks. They taught me a history about myself.

Those stories my family shared with me I have drawn upon to share with people around the world.

THE WELL

They are the stories upon which all the Logan books have been based. *The Well* is another such story. It is a story told by David Logan about his boyhood. Those readers familiar with my other books about the Logan family—*Roll of Thunder*, *Hear My Cry*; *Let the Circle Be Unbroken*; *The Road to Memphis*; and others—will recognize David as the father of Cassie, Stacey, Christopher-John, and Little Man. Just as my father and other members of my family passed on family history through the stories, so does David. It is David's story, but in telling it, it becomes Cassie's and her brothers' too. It becomes part of the Logan family saga.

The Well

Charlie Simms was always mean, and that's the truth of it. Thing is we never knew just how mean he was until that year back when all the wells in our part of Mississippi went dry. All the wells except ours, that is. We was blessed. We had good sweet water in a well that ran deep. Most folks said our land must've been sitting on an underground lake, if there is such a thing. Well, I don't know about that. All I know is that well of ours never went dry. Now some folks wouldn't've shared their water, but Mama, and Papa too, weren't those kind of folks. They believed in sharing what they had, and they tried to teach us boys—my brothers Mitchell and Kevin, Hammer, and me—the same thing; but sometimes it was real hard to do, to share, especially when some of the folks you had to share with were folks the likes of Charlie Simms and his family, folks who hated your guts.

Our two families, the Logans and the Simmses, had never much gotten along. What with the Simmses living less than a mile or so from us on that forty-acre spot of land they tenant-farmed, and we sitting on our own two hundred acres, there was always likely to be trouble, and there was. Now this was back before my papa went and bought that second two hundred acres; but still that two hundred acres we had then, that was a lot, and the Simmses didn't like it—that we had when they didn't. They didn't like it one bit. That was part of the trouble between us. Other part of the trouble was that we were coloured and they were white. Fact of the matter was we ain't never had much use for the Simmses, and they ain't never had much use for us either; but seeing that we couldn't hardly afford trouble with them, Papa said best thing to do was try and stay out of their way much as we could. He said it was better to mind our business, let them mind theirs, and just walk away if they tried to start something.

I heeded his words. My brother Hammer didn't.

During those dry days the Simmses, like a lot of other folks, took their water from the Creek Rosa Lee.

But then things got so bad that even the Rosa Lee began to muddy and dry, and folks who had never been to our place for water before began to show up. Coloured folks, and white folks too.

Even the Simmses.

It was just after dawn the morning Charlie and his brother Ed-Rose pulled up in their wagon with two big barrels setting on it. Hammer and me, we'd just come from the barn after milking some of the cows when we seen them. Hammer was walking ahead of me carrying a full milk bucket in each hand. Me, I was only carrying one bucket because I was on a crutch that summer. I had fallen from a tree and busted up my leg, so I had on a cast, had a limp, and I moved slow. Now I wasn't any happier than Hammer to see the Simmses, but I was ready to act civil and say good morning. Not Hammer. First thing out of his mouth: "What y'all doing up here?"

Charlie Simms, no more than fourteen at the time, held the reins to their mules. Ed-Rose, maybe a year or so younger, sat beside him. Charlie stared down at Hammer and me and didn't answer. Ed-Rose stared too, but at least he spoke. "Where's your folks?" he asked.

"Don't you worry 'bout where they are," said Hammer. "I'm the one standing here." Hammer couldn't have been more than thirteen, and I was three years younger than that. I was kind of a quiet boy, and Hammer in his way was too, except he always spoke like a man, a man sure of himself. A man sure of himself even in front of white folks.

"You gettin' smart with me, boy?" asked Ed-Rose.

Now back then white folks ruled everything. A white man said jump, and most black folks did. White man said move out the way, and most black folks did. White folks could say and do what they wanted, just because they ruled things; because just one word out of them against a black person—man or woman, or even a child—and that black man or that black woman or that child could be hanging from a tree, even just for mouthing off. One word. Hammer knew it. I knew it too. Still, Hammer said what he figured to say. He didn't jump. We hadn't been brought up that way.

Without a word Hammer turned and stepped back to the barn. He set the buckets on the ground, next to the door, and came back. Hands free now, he stuffed them into his pockets. "I'm not the one sitting on a wagon with two empty water barrels," he smart-mouthed. "I'm not the one sitting on someone else's land. And I'm sure not the one gotta be answering questions."

At that, Charlie Simms threw the reins aside and jumped up. "Look-a-here, you smart-talkin' nigger—"

"Hammer! David!" Mama opened the side door and came out. She took one look at the Simmses, at us, and knew what was going on. "Why ain't y'all told me we had folks callin'?"

Hammer didn't say a word. Me either.

Mama came over to the dirt driveway and looked again at the Simmses. "Y'all come to get water?"

"Yeah," they said, showing her no respect, neither one saying "yes, ma'am" to her. That made my blood boil; that was my mama they were speaking to. But I said nothing. I didn't want trouble.

Mama nodded towards the well. "There it is," she said. "Y'alls welcomed to it. Get much as you need."

Charlie and Ed-Rose didn't move. They didn't mutter a word. They kept their eyes on Hammer and me.

Mama watched them watching us. "You boys, David and Hammer, y'all come with me," she said. "Breakfast 'bout ready. Hammer, get them buckets and come on in the house."

"In a minute, Mama," Hammer said real quiet-like, and his eyes slanted down in that cold way they could. "Right now, I figure to stay here and give Ed-Rose and Charlie a hand with *our* water."

Mama glanced again at Ed-Rose and Charlie, then again at Hammer. "I figure they can manage," she said.

"I'm staying," Hammer said.

Now Mama was a tall woman, big-boned and strong; she was taller, bigger than my papa. Well, she put her hands on her hips and gave Hammer a don't-mess-with-me kind of look. "I'll get my strap to ya, boy, you back talk me again. Now get them buckets and come on!" With that, without waiting for another word from Hammer, she turned and headed back for the house.

Hammer eyed the Simmses, took his hands from his pockets and went back to the barn for the buckets. He picked them up, cut another look at the Simmses and walked across the yard to the house. I looked back at the Simmses too, still on their wagon, then, leaning on my crutch and carrying my milk bucket, followed Hammer. Neither of the Simmses stepped down from the wagon until the door closed behind us. We stepped inside and found Mama standing by the door, whipping strap in hand. Hammer eyed the strap without a word and walked on to the pantry and put the milk buckets on the sideboard. Mama watched him, then hung the strap on a nail beside the door. None of us said a word.

Now at that time the kitchen wasn't part of the main house. A body had to walk down a covered outside walkway to a separate room. That's the way folks used to build houses in them days, with a separate cooking place to keep the fire danger down. Well, my Grandma Rachel and my Aunt Callie—that was Mama's sister—had been down at the kitchen cooking, and they come in just about then bringing in the breakfast food: pot of steaming butter grits, long pan of hot biscuits, sausages and bacon, eggs, and pear preserves. Nobody ever accused us Logans of not eating good at our table! Anyways, Ma Rachel took one look at the three of us, set the food on the table, stared us down, and demanded to know what was the matter. "Y'all tell me what it is," she said.

I watched Ma Rachel with a bit of caution and hoped Mama wouldn't tell her. Everybody knew Ma Rachel wasn't very partial to white folks, especially not the Simmses. Not only that, but Ma Rachel was a bit touched in the head. Everybody knew that too.

"Nothin', Mama," Mama answered. "Jus' folks comin' for water."

"What folks this time?" questioned Ma Rachel.

"Oh . . . nobody particular," said Hammer. "Just them Simmses."

If looks could cut, Mama's would've done it. She

cut a look at Hammer, then said to Ma, "Now don't go upsettin' yo'self. They jus' come for water. They be gone in a minute."

"Yeah, they come for water all right," snapped Hammer. "And Mama jus' up and let 'em have it, much as they want."

I cut Hammer a look myself, wishing he'd watch his mouth because I knew Mama wasn't going to let him keep getting away with smarting off. Like always, being Hammer, he paid no attention.

Mama turned to him, and I was kind of surprised when all she did was talk to him. "Now God done blessed us with that water, son, and long's I'm here, what we been blessed with, we're gonna share long's other folks in need."

Ma Rachel walked over to the window and looked out to the well. I moved right behind her, keeping my eyes on her. She put her hands on her hips and shook her head. "Other folks don't mean the Simmses. You too generous, girl. First they comes and takes our water; next thing ya know, they be coming t' take the land. You too free with what God done give ya, Caroline. Way too free."

"That may be, but long's I got breath in my body and that water's in that ground, I'm gonna give it."

Ma Rachel turned. "Not long's I live!" she said,

and all of a sudden lunged for the shotgun over the door.

I let go of my crutch and laid hold of the shotgun too and tried to wrestle it from her. "Naw, Ma Rachel!" I shouted. "Naw!"

"Ah, Lordy!" cried Aunt Callie as she and Mama rushed over. "Ah, Lordy!" Aunt Callie said again just as Mama snatched the shotgun from both Ma Rachel and me.

"Ain't gonna be no shootin'," Mama said, not a rise of anger in her voice. "Ain't gonna be no shootin'."

"I ain't wantin' them white folks on this land!" Ma Rachel cried. "They come on this land, I'm gonna find me 'nother place t' go! Ya hear me, Caroline? I'm gonna find me 'nother place t' go!"

Mama sighed and placed the shotgun back over the door, then she put her arm around her mama. Ma Rachel was a small woman, and standing there with Mama's arms around her, it looked almost as if she was the child. After a bit my grandma pulled away from Mama and sat down in a rocker by the window.

"They done took my name!" she moaned. "They done took my name. They done took it, and I wants them 'way from here!"

I was watching her and I was thinking, here we

were nearly some ten years into what folks called the twentieth century, but Ma Rachel's mind was still in the last century dwelling on those days when she was a slave.

Mama tried to give her some comfort and Aunt Callie said, "Jus' rest yo'self, Mama. They'll be gone soon. Don't fret yo'self now. They'll be gone soon."

"Not soon enough for me," said Hammer.

Mama turned as if she'd just about had it with him. The only thing saved him was a knock on the door. It was Mr Clinton Melbourne and his son, George. "Come to get some water, that be all right with y'all," said Mr Melbourne.

"Help yo'self," said Mama. "Y'alls welcome to it."

Mr Melbourne nodded, his way of giving thanks. Looking a bit embarrassed, he nodded a second time, then he and his son went back to their wagon, unloaded their empty barrels and took them over to the well. There they stood waiting for Charlie and Ed-Rose to finish drawing water. The Melbournes, they were nice folks. They always treated us fair; still, we didn't forget that they were white and we were coloured. We figured they didn't either.

Ma Rachel stared out the window at the Melbournes and the Simmses and shook her head. "More white folks on our land," she muttered. Then she repeated herself. "Ya too generous with these folks, Caroline, after what they done! Ya too generous!"

"I can agree with that," said Hammer.

"You hush, boy!" said Mama. "You and David, y'all go on and get washed up for breakfast. Go on, now!"

Hammer scowled, but he obeyed. He went to the back porch and I followed. We found our cousin Halton already there, washing off the morning sweat after working in the fields. Halton was Aunt Callie's boy, and he was staying with us now. Halton was near grown, about the same age as my oldest brother, Mitchell, and he had himself a sturdy build, like a boxer. He grinned at us. Halton always seemed to be grinning. He was just one of those folks naturally had a sunshiny way about them; nothing much ever seemed to bother him. "What y'all little scounds up to?" he asked.

"Jus' come to wash up," said Hammer.

Halton nodded. "What was all that commotion goin' on in there?"

I told him.

He grunted. "Them Simmses ain't never been nothin' but trouble. Y'all little scounds stay clear of 'em."

"Easier said than done," said Hammer.

"Well, y'all do it anyway," said Halton; then he grinned his big wide grin again. "'Nough of them," he said, and threw out his wash water. "Y'all get y'allselves washed and hurry up 'bout it! I'm past ready to eat!" He locked his great arms around the back of each of our necks, gave a friendly squeeze and laughed, then let us go and went into the house.

"Brother, you aiming for a whipping?" I asked Hammer soon as Halton was inside. "You keep messing with Mama and you gonna get one, sure enough."

Hammer took up the soap Mama had made, dipped water from a bucket and poured it into the wash pan, and lathered up.

"Well?" I said. I wanted an answer.

Hammer finished his washing and rinsed off his hands before he answered me. "Whipping be well worth it, I could run them Simmses 'way from here."

"Can't do it," I said. "They white, we coloured. Running them off would just mean trouble. And you know what Papa says, you gotta weigh what kind of trouble you gonna take on. Seems to me, sharing water when we got plenty ain't a good enough reason for trouble."

"Maybe you think not," said Hammer. "Me, I

agree with Ma Rachel. White folks, 'specially the Simmses, got no business on our land."

I was quiet a moment, then spoke low. "You know Ma Rachel kinda touched in the head . . . 'specially when it comes to white folks."

"Then I 'spect maybe I am too. They got no business here." He walked down to the end of the porch and stood there staring out. I washed my hands and watched him. As I dried my hands on the porch towel, he turned and came back.

"They gone?" I asked.

He nodded. "Nice of them to thank us, wasn't it?" He met my eyes, opened the back door, and went inside.

I didn't follow him this time. Instead I hobbled on my crutch to the end of the porch. The Melbournes were now drawing water from the well. Like Hammer said, the Simmses were gone, but I knew that as long as this dry spell lasted, they'd be back. Knowing that, I looked up at the sky and prayed for rain. Lots of it. I prayed it would rain so folks wouldn't have to be coming to our well. I prayed it would rain so the Simmses wouldn't have to come here again, because I figured if they did come, sooner or later, there was going to be trouble.

*   *   *

Breakfast that morning was kind of quiet. Hammer was in a mood; so was Ma Rachel. I ain't had much to say myself. Aunt Callie had gone on home, but Halton was at the table, and it was him and Mama who done most of the talking. Papa and Mitchell and Kevin, they usually done a great bit of the talking at the table, great part of the laughing too, but they were away now doing lumbering along the Natchez Trace. They'd been gone for more than a month. The last couple of years they'd been going away to do lumbering work to get money for taxes and for some of the things Papa and Mama wanted our family to have, including more land.

Since they'd been away, not only had Halton been staying with us to help out, but Aunt Callie had been spending a lot more of her time here too. Now Aunt Callie and her husband, my Uncle Lawrence, and their children lived on our place, but they had their own house, their own fields, on the other side of the woods. Most days Aunt Callie was up to our house anyway a couple of times a day to see about Ma Rachel and visit with her and Mama, but with Papa, Kevin, and Mitchell gone, she was visiting even more. She and Halton and Uncle Lawrence called themselves keeping watch on us.

That was all well and good, having them keep

watch, but far as I was concerned, Papa and my brothers had been gone long enough lumbering on that Natchez Trace. I was missing them, and I knew Hammer was too. I figured it was high time they came back. Mama kept saying any day now they'd be home, and they would stay a while when they came home too. They would stay and watch out for us themselves and help us out with the farm work. Soon, she said, soon. But she'd been saying that for more than a week, and I don't even think she really knew when they'd finally come walking up the road.

After breakfast it was Hammer's and my job to take the cows to get water. Now back then our family was considered rather prosperous, for folks black or white. We had ourselves the two hundred acres, cotton fields, fruit orchards, and a garden. Mama had herself a buggy and Papa had himself one of the finest stallions in the county. We also had ourselves plenty of livestock—hogs, chickens, guineas, ducks, horses, mules, goats and cows. We had some thirty cows and calves. Fact, we had so many cows, we had to graze half of them in the pasture behind the barn and the other half down near the pond. Because everything was drying up, the pond was nearly dried out too, but there was still enough water for the cows to get themselves a drink. Each morning we'd take the cows down to the pond and then bring them back again 'round the time the sun set. Well, this particular morning when we gone to take the cows down, we found it so near to dry, we decided to take them on to the Creek Rosa Lee. Even though folks couldn't drink the muddy water any more, leastways maybe the cows could.

On the way to the creek we met up with John Henry Berry. John Henry was the same age as Hammer, and the two were good friends. "'Ey there, John Henry," Hammer and I both said.

"'Ey, y'all," said John Henry, and gave his bony cow a swat to push her on. "Y'all headed to the Rosa Lee?"

"That's right," said Hammer.

"Then I walk 'long with ya."

"Fine," said Hammer, and we kept on going.

When we got down to the Rosa Lee, we found Charlie and Ed-Rose along with Dewberry Wallace, a close friend of theirs, and Mr Melbourne's boy, George, watering their cows. With them was Joe McCalister, a few years older than the other boys, and black. Altogether, they had some seven cows, and here we come with our fifteen, plus John Henry's one.

THE WELL

It didn't look good.

"'Ey, there, Hammer, David, John Henry!" cried Joe with his good nature.

"'Ey, Joe," I returned, and Hammer and John Henry gave a nod. Charlie and Ed-Rose and Dewberry gave us a mean look. George Melbourne moved his family's cow away from the others. Hammer and me, we headed our cows towards the water. John Henry and his cow came along.

"Now just hold it right there!" ordered Dewberry. "Hold it right there! There ain't water 'nough here for all them cows!"

Charlie laughed. "Don't tell me y'all niggers gotta come to the creek now t' water your animals. Thought y'all had a pond t' water from."

"Yeah, we got a pond," answered Hammer. "Got some fifteen more cows too, to water from that pond. Figured to water these here from the Rosa Lee, yeah, like everybody else. Figured to save that pond water for our other cows."

I stood there not saying a word, figuring, though, we was about to die. John Henry looked as if he was figuring the same.

The white boys looked at each other, then Charlie spoke again. "Y'all Logans some mighty uppity niggers, ya know that? Think y'all good's white folks 'cause you got a little land and some livestock.''

"And don't forget . . . we got water too," said Hammer, rubbing salt into Charlie Simms' already festering soul. "Water y'all gotta come to us to get.''

"Well don't y'all go gettin' so prideful 'bout that water, nigger! Maybe one day you won't have it! Maybe one day y'all'll find somethin' dead floatin' in it!''

I thought my heart was going to burst, it was beating so fast and furious. I could see me or mine floating in that water. I was angry too that they were calling us by *that* word again. It was a galling word, an insulting word that made my blood boil, but a word I had to take because that was just the way white folks talked to us. Maybe some figured no insult by it, but to me it was always a stinging insult, and I stored that insult in my memory.

"So y'all niggers get!" ordered Dewberry, saying that word again. "Y'all ain't waterin' no nigger cows down here t'day!''

"Yeah," said Ed-Rose, "go on and water 'em from that pond of y'alls!''

George Melbourne ain't said a thing. But Joe McCalister—bless his heart—he sure enough did. "Now jus' wait-a minute, Mr Ed-Rose!" he exclaimed. "Them cows be needin' water and God ain't gonna smile on a body turn 'way His dumb creatures needin' water!"

Ed-Rose, Dewberry, George, and Charlie too, all looked at Joe. Now one thing about Joe McCalister was that he was what some folks would call not so bright. He had a good heart, though, and most folks cared about him, and even if they didn't, they put up with him. Joe was the kind of person who could speak his mind and folks wouldn't take offence, I suppose because folks figured whatever Joe had to say wasn't worth taking offence about.

"Now ya gots t' let 'em drink, Mr Ed-Rose," Joe went on, "'cause God, He done put this water here for everybody and—"

"Joe, shut up," said Charlie. And Joe shut up. Then Charlie turned back to Hammer and me. "Y'all get," he said.

"Yeah," said Dewberry.

"And get now," added Ed-Rose, "'fore we go and forget jus' how y'all s'pose t' be some of God's dumb creatures too."

Hammer didn't say anything back to any of them. He just looked at me, swatted one of the cows with his switch and headed the cows upstream. John Henry with his cow came too. I looked back at the Simmses, at Dewberry and George, and wondered if they would follow. They didn't. Once we were out of sight and hearing distance of them, John Henry stopped his cow and he said, "Ya know ya crazy, don't ya, Hammer? Ya crazy to go talkin' to these white folks like that! Don't ya know these white folks'll kill ya?"

Hammer looked at John Henry. "I 'spect I do," he said, then he moved on and headed the cows straight into the muddy waters of the Rosa Lee.

John Henry Berry shook his head. "Crazy," he muttered. "Plain, downright crazy. I stay friends with you, I hope you don't end up gettin' me hung."

I looked at John Henry and knew how he was feeling; but Hammer was just Hammer, and I followed after him. So did John Henry.

I suspect the Simmses and Dewberry Wallace knew once we were out of their sight that we watered our cows in the Rosa Lee. I 'spect they knew that, but they didn't come after us. I was nervous about watering those cows in that creek and John Henry was too, but Hammer stayed his time, letting the cows drink their muddy fill. Then, after what seemed like an eternity to this David Logan, he finally turned the cows towards home.

*   *   *

Later that same week Hammer and me were walking the road towards home when we seen a wagon hung over in a ditch with one of its wheels off. All the contents from that wagon were strewn over the ground, and Charlie Simms was in the ditch knelt beside the wagon looking all sick about that missing wheel. Then he seen us, and he hollered, "Y'all up there! Come give me a hand!"

Hammer looked around, first one way, then the other; then he said, "You talkin' to us?"

"Don't see no other niggers standing up there," countered Charlie.

Hammer clenched his fists. I stepped forward. I wasn't intending to see us mixed into trouble about this. "I'll give you a hand," I said.

Charlie Simms sneered at me. "What kinda help you gonna be? You here with a busted leg! I want that boy yonder to get under this wagon and push it up."

I glanced back at Hammer and could see he was getting mighty vexed. "I can do it!" I said. "Busted leg got nothin' to do with my back."

"David!" Hammer snapped at me. "Don't you do it! *Don't you do it!* I ain't gonna help ya none!"

"I ain't askin' ya to!" I snapped back. Now I had my pride just like Hammer did, but I knew that if we didn't help Charlie out, the trouble that ran between us was just going to get worse; so I limped to the back of the wagon, laid down my crutch, and hefted the low end of the wagon, while Charlie tried to get the wheel back on. "Hurry up!" I said, because that wagon was heavy.

Charlie, though, seemed to be taking his time. "Don't rush me, boy. I get it on when I get it on."

"I can't hold it much longer!"

He laughed. "Thought you was the one had such a strong back." He seemed to be toying with the wheel when all he had to do was slip it on the axle. I waited maybe a minute, maybe two, an eternity it seemed to me, and he still didn't have that wheel on.

"I gotta let it go!" I finally yelled out. "It's too heavy!"

"You do and I'll—"

The wagon slammed down and ole Charlie fell back with the wheel into the ditch. "I told you I couldn't hold it," I said, and reached for my crutch. Charlie rolled the wheel aside, scrambled up from the ditch, and, before I could step aside, he laid his back hand across my jaw and knocked me down.

That was the worst thing he could've done.

Hammer, who hadn't lifted a finger to help me with the wagon, dashed across the road and tore into

Charlie Simms, knocking him back into the ditch. Hammer fell on top of him and pounded at his face. Charlie finally was able to push him off and tried to climb back on to the road. But Hammer wasn't finished with him yet. He reached for his arm and turned him around.

"Hammer!" I yelled. "Leave him be!" I attempted to pull myself up so I could try and stop Hammer, knowing all the while that when Hammer got this mad, there was no stopping him, for Hammer had a temper like a fire raging. But I kept yelling at him anyway to stop. He paid no attention to me. He hit Charlie one more time with an iron fist and laid him out flat. This time, though, Charlie didn't get up. He didn't move.

"Get up!" Hammer ordered.

Charlie still didn't move.

"I said get up, you no count excuse for a snake! Get up!"

But Charlie just lay there.

I caught on to the back of the wagon and finally managed to pull myself to my feet. I limped over to the ditch and studied Charlie, then turned to Hammer. "Lord, Hammer," I said, "he done hit his head on that rock and . . . I think he's dead!"

Hammer stepped back and only now unclenched

his fists; his face was showing no remorse at what he'd done. If he was scared, he wasn't showing that either. But I was sure enough scared, and I was ready to get out of there. I stared down at Charlie. "What we gonna do, Hammer! What we gonna do?"

Hammer stared down at Charlie too and shrugged. "'Spect there's nothin' we can do now, is there?"

I just looked at him and wondered how long it would be before we both got hung. After all, young as we were, we knew enough to know that black boys of any age didn't go around hitting white boys of any age. Black boy hit a white boy, black man hit a white man, he could get hung in a flick of a horse's tail, and that's just the way things were. I ain't hardly lying when I say this David Logan was mighty scared.

It was just about then Halton came along. He hollered at us, not seeing Charlie lying there in the ditch. "What y'all little scounds doin'?" he said, face in that grin of his until he came around that wagon and saw for himself what we were doing. He took one look and the smile was gone. Without even asking what had happened, he said, "Let's go! We gotta get outa here!"

I asked him what about Charlie.

"One of you done hit him?"

"Yeah, I did," said Hammer, owning up to it without a bit of hesitating; no bragging in his words, no sorrow either, just fact. "I did."

"Then there's no time for talkin' now. Come on! We gotta get outa here! Quick, now!"

I hobbled around the wagon and started up the road.

"No!" Halton said. "Through the woods! David, hold on to your crutch and get on my back!"

"But—"

"Do what I tell ya, boy! We gotta fly!"

I said nothing else. Halton knelt down and before I could climb on his back, he flung me on to it. "Hold tight," he ordered, and took off with me across the road and into the woods on the other side. Halton, even with me on his back, ran like the wind through the pines, and Hammer was right behind. We said nothing all the way home, but all that long way all I could think about was Charlie Simms was dead, and that maybe soon Hammer would be too. I was more scared than I had ever been in my life.

Not until we reached the back porch did Halton put me down. Mama came from the house, broom in her hand, took one look at us and knew something was wrong. "What is it?" she demanded.

Halton tried to catch his breath, but there wasn't time. "Hammer, he done hit Charlie Simms."

"Yeah, and I'd hit him again."

Mama's dark eyes went darker, and she stared at Hammer. "You . . . you done what?"

"He hit David," said Hammer sullenly, as if that was supposed to answer all her questions. "He won't be hitting him again."

"He ain't movin', Aunt Caroline," said Halton. "I come 'long after Hammer done laid Charlie out. He ain't movin'. He laying in a ditch up there near the crossroads."

"Oh, dear Jesus," Mama said in a voice suddenly gone quiet. She looked out across the fields to the woods. She closed her eyes for several moments, as if she was praying, then she opened them again. "You check him, Halton?"

Halton shook his head. "I ain't touched him. I just got David and Hammer, and we got outa there." He was quiet a moment, still breathing heavily, then he added, "Aunt Caroline . . . when I was coming up past the white folks' school, I seen the sheriff. Him being down in these parts, he'll most likely know soon."

Mama bit at her lip, then she nodded and put the broom aside. "All right, all right," she said, as if making up her mind about something. "Halton, you take Hammer and you hide him in the woods there near your Uncle Paul-Edward's praying rock. David, you come with me."

"What you gonna do, Aunt Caroline?" asked Halton.

"Gonna go check on that boy. Now y'all hurry, and Hammer—" She took a firm hold of Hammer's shoulders. "You mind what Halton tell ya to do. Ya hear me now?"

"I hear."

"Now go on, both of ya, and don't y'all come back here 'til I sends for ya!"

With that, Hammer and Halton dashed across the yard past the smokehouse, past the garden, through the orchard, and across the pasture towards the woods and Papa's praying rock. Mama ran back inside the house to check on Ma Rachel taking her afternoon nap, then, with me trailing behind her fast as I could, she hurried across the side yard and around the barn to the barnyard and called for Raindrop, the mare that always pulled her buggy. But Mama didn't take the time to hitch Raindrop to the buggy this day. Instead, she simply bridled her, helped me up, then got on herself and turned Raindrop towards the wooded path Halton, Hammer and I had just travelled. She said it was quicker than the road. When we reached the wagon, we didn't get down. Instead, we went around it and looked over into the ditch.

Charlie wasn't there.

"David, you sure this here where you left him?" Mama asked.

"Yes, ma'am, right there! He hit his head on that rock yonder!"

Mama sighed. "Well, he not there now."

"You . . . you figure they done found him already?"

"I . . . I 'spect."

"Well . . . then what we do now, Mama?" I asked.

"We go home . . . and we wait. They'll be comin' soon." She looked up and down the road, into the woods on either side, then reining the horse around, gave Raindrop a click and a nudge, and we tore up the road towards home.

When we got to the house, Joe McCalister was standing by the well with Mr Tom Bee, a neighbour of ours. "'Ey, how do there, Miz Caroline?" greeted Joe. "David, how you, boy?"

Mama reined in Raindrop and got down. She helped me to the ground, then turned towards the well.

"We was just waitin' here for y'all t' get back," said

Mr Tom Bee. "We done knocked on the door, but ain't nobody answered. Figured it'd be all right with y'all we gone ahead and get some water, but we—" On a sudden Mr Tom Bee stopped his talking and looked close at Mama. "Somethin' wrong, Miz Caroline?"

"Everything's wrong," answered Mama. "Everything."

"What you mean?"

Mama took in a deep, deep breath. "Hammer. My boy, Hammer, he done gone and hit that white boy, Charlie Simms. Knocked him out. He done hit his head on a rock, and we figurin' him t' be dead—"

"Dead!" cried Mr Tom Bee.

"That's right, dead. David and me, we jus' gone t' see 'bout him, but . . . but he ain't there where Hammer done knocked him out. S'pose his family done found him already. Reckon they gonna come soon for my Hammer. Oh, Lord, how come my Paul-Edward ain't here? They gonna come!"

Joe laughed. "What ya talkin' 'bout, Miz Caroline? That Charlie Simms, he ain't dead!"

"*What?* Boy, what you sayin'?"

"That's sure the truth!" said Mr Tom Bee. "We jus' done seen that boy Charlie over there front of the white folks' school. Seen him when we was on our way here. Him and his brother, they was jus' standin' up there talkin' t' the sheriff—"

"The sheriff?" said Mama.

"Yes, ma'am, that's right. Sheriff and them, they was doin' some talkin', but we ain't stopped to jaw with 'em none. They was lookin' mighty serious, and ya know we ain't had no mind to go messin' in white folks' business."

Mama nodded. She closed her eyes and her lips moved, but no sound came out.

"Lordy, Miz Caroline!" said Joe. "Ya all right?"

For a moment there, Mama didn't open her eyes or say a word. Then she took a deep breath, opened her eyes to the heavens, and said, "Thank ya, Lord, that boy he ain't dead. He ain't dead!"

"They not gonna come now, huh, Mama?" I said.

She put her hand on my shoulder. "Naw, child, they still gonna come all right. Your brother done hit himself a white boy. Yeah, they still gonna come. But the Lord, He done stepped in and give the breath of life back to Charlie Simms. He done give it back! Now I know He gonna watch out after my Hammer too!" She took her hand away and hurried towards the house. "David, you come with me!"

"What you gonna do, Mama?" I asked, hurrying behind her fast as I could with my gimpy leg.

"Gonna cook me some molasses bread!"

I stopped. I was figuring Mama had gone crazy. "Molasses bread?" I said.

"That's right. I been knowin' that sheriff since he was a boy, so you come on now and you can give me a hand! We gotta hurry! We gotta hurry!"

I turned and looked at Mr Tom Bee and Joe McCalister. Both of them was looking puzzled as I was by the way Mama was acting.

"Uh . . . Miz Caroline," called Mr Tom Bee, "ya wantin' us to stay on up here a while?"

"No, suh, thank ya!" Mama hollered back, still moving. "Y'all get y'alls water and y'all go on! Best no full-grown menfolks be standin' up here whens they get here! That'll jus' mean more trouble. Y'all get y'alls water and go on now! We'll be all right! I knows what I gotta do! David, hurry up, boy! We ain't got much time!"

She was running now. She ran onto the porch, not even looking back, just expecting me to follow. I glanced around again at Mr Tom Bee. He was all frowned up, looking worried. He didn't give me a sign what to do, what to think, so I limped on across the yard, and followed my mama to the kitchen house.

It wasn't too long after that the sheriff showed up.

Sheriff Peterson Rankins, his name was. He was a large-sized fella, sandy hair and a moustache, looked like he was always burned by the sun. He'd been up to our place before; he'd even come for water. Mama and Papa, they was always cordial to him, but they ain't never got close, not like some folks did with him. Mama and Papa, they always kept their distance. They said it was best that way. Anyways, he came to our place riding his stallion, stepped down from his horse, and went over to the well. We were looking out the window watching him, waiting for him. He didn't bother to come up to the house and ask if he could get himself a drink. He just took off the lid that covered the well and pulled himself up a bucket.

Mama heaved a heavy sigh and thanked the Lord Mr Tom Bee and Joe were gone. Then she said to me, "All right now, David, you watch out for your Ma Rachel. She nappin' now, but she wake up, you make sure she don't see that sheriff and make sure she don't come out. You hear me?"

"Yes, ma'am," I said. "I'll take care of her."

Mama nodded, set her jaw, pulled the door open, then stepped out. I watched her from the darkness of the room. The sheriff took his drink and looked up. Mama stopped right where she was on the stone doorstep. The sheriff, he took his full of water, poured what he didn't have a thirst for back in the bucket, and came over. "Well, how do there, Caroline?" he asked.

"Jus' fine," Mama answered. "Water there still sweet?"

The sheriff glanced back at the well. "Finest water in the county. Always said so. Y'all blessed, Caroline. Without that water don't know what half the folks 'round here woulda done." Mama gave a nod and he came on up the side yard and stopped just before he reached the step. "I understand Paul-Edward and your oldest boys, they away lumberin'."

"Yes, suh, that's right," Mama said.

The sheriff grunted, then got on with his business. "S'pose ya know how come I'm here."

Mama just looked at him for a moment, then she said, "All I knows is what my boy David in there done told me."

"David?" said the sheriff. "Ya mean to tell me he still 'round here?"

"He still 'round," said Mama.

"Then you tell him t' get on out here."

"He taking care of Ma Rachel. Best we talk, jus' you and me."

The sheriff met her eyes, and his eyes narrowed

down. He waited a moment, then he said, "Where's that Hammer?"

"Hammer? Don't rightly know where that boy is."

"You better know. After what he gone and done, you sure 'nough better know."

Mama stood straight and tall. "What he done?"

"Thought you said David done told ya."

"He told me his side, but he ain't told me what you gonna say."

The sheriff sighed, took off his hat, and mopped his brow with a large handkerchief, then he mopped the sweat from the inside of his hatband. "Charlie Simms—that's Old Mr McCalister Simms' boy—he jus' got hit in the head. His brother Ed-Rose come and got me. I gone over to the Simms place and Old Mr McCalister 'bout fit to be tied." He stuffed the handkerchief back in his pocket, slapped the hat back on his head, and stared direct at Mama.

Mama waited, still as a windless day.

"Charlie told me your boys, Hammer and David, done half-killed him with a side of lumber."

"The boy, he all right?"

"Yeah. He got some bruises, but I figure his feelings smartin' more'n them bruises."

"You done said Charlie Simms said both Hammer *and* David done hit him?"

"Yeah, that's right."

Mama frowned and didn't say anything.

"That the story you heard?"

"That what he done told ya, then ya got no call t' believe what my boys done told me."

"And jus' what was that?"

"You gonna take my boys' words over them Simmses?"

"You jus' tell me."

Mama glanced back towards the kitchen. "You don't mind, Sheriff Rankins, I got my supper on cookin'. Ma Rachel, she been feelin' poorly, so I ain't got nobody t' watch out for it. You mind if I see t' my food? You mind if we talk by the kitchen?"

"Well, I s'pose no matter what your boys done gone and done, you folks still gotta eat. Go on. Lead the way."

Mama nodded. She left the doorway and stepped along the stones that led to the back porch. I left the window, checked on Ma Rachel, seen her still napping in her room, then I took off to the pantry where I could watch what was going on at the kitchen house. The sheriff and Mama stood on the walk-way in front of the open kitchen door. The smell of molasses bread was strong. The sheriff sniffed the air and looked at Mama. "What's that I smell cookin'?"

"Jus' my molasses bread," said Mama. "'Scuse me, but I best check on it 'fore it burn. Please take yourself a seat on the bench there."

With that, she gone into the kitchen house. The sheriff, he sniffed the air again, then sat down, took off his hat, and laid it on the bench. He crossed his legs and looked out across the yard. He seemed right calm, not at all hurried about taking Hammer and me in. There was a window in that kitchen, and I could see Mama taking out the long pans of molasses bread and setting them on the side shelf right next to the door. The sheriff could see her too.

"Ya know I ain't had molasses bread in I don't know when—I 'spect not since our cook, Aunt Cora, died more'n a year ago. Now that old nigra woman could sure 'nough cook! My wife, well, she jus' ain't got the touch for cookin' like old Aunt Cora done had. We got ourselves a young nigra gal come up to help her out, but she ain't much got the touch neither."

Mama came out of the kitchen and nodded, as if the sheriff not having any molasses bread was of some great concern to her, but she said nothing. The sheriff glanced through the door at those great pans of bread cooling on the sideboard and cleared his throat. "It sure do look mighty good."

"Well, let me get you a piece," Mama said, and went back into the kitchen. She cut a sizeable square of the bread, plopped a heaping spoonful of newly churned butter on top, and took it to the sheriff, along with a large glass of fresh buttermilk. The sheriff thanked her, took a hefty bite of the molasses bread and butter, and smiled. Then he cleared his throat and looked at Mama. "So what your boys done said happened, Caroline?"

"Well, 'cording to my boy David, him and Hammer was walking 'long the road when they run 'cross Charlie Simms. The Simms boy, he needed help putting a wheel back on his wagon, and he done asked them to help him out. David, he done held the wagon up for Charlie Simms to put the wheel back on, but he done told the Simms boy he couldn't hold it long and that he was gonna hafta let it go, and that's what he done—he let it go. Well, Charlie Simms, he done hit him for letting it go. Hit him and knocked him down, off his crutch—you know my David, he done broke his leg a few weeks back, and he been having to use a crutch ever since. Well, anyways, David said that's what Charlie Simms done to him, and Hammer done beat him for it—with his fists, mind ya. He ain't used no side of lumber, nothin' else, jus' his fists. He hit Charlie Simms with his fists, and Charlie Simms

done fell back on a rock and hit his head, and that's
what done knocked him out."

The sheriff grunted and finished his molasses
bread. He wiped the plate clean. Mama waited. He
drank his buttermilk. Mama waited. Finally he put
the plate down on the bench, and sighed. "That was
sure mighty good, Caroline. Mighty good."

"Thank ya."

"I sure wouldn't mind takin' a piece home, let my
wife have a taste."

"There's plenty," said Mama. "Ya welcome to it."

The sheriff nodded his gratitude. Mama stood
there, still waiting. The sheriff sighed and looked at
her. "Now, Caroline, you know I can't jus' go 'lowing
Hammer to go 'round hitting a white boy. Hammer
and David, they gotta pay for what they done."

"David, he ain't touched Charlie Simms."

"Well . . . that's David's story."

"David don't lie."

"Well, that may be, but I can't hardly go believing
him over Charlie, can I now?"

"That's up to you, I reckon."

The sheriff was silent again, studying on the matter. He drank the last of his buttermilk and set the
glass down beside the plate. Then he got up. "I'll tell
ya what I'll do. I'll go talk to Old Man McCalister

Simms and see if I can't get him not to press charges on this thing. I'll see if maybe he'll accept Hammer and David working for him for a spell. I think he'll see he can come out ahead that way, 'stead of me takin' them boys to jail."

Mama nodded. "We'd be obliged if you can work it out that way. We ain't wantin' our boys in no jail."

"Well, fact of the matter is you and Paul-Edward, y'all been doin' a mighty Christian thing here, lettin' folks use your water like you been. Lotta folks couldn't've made it, they couldn't count on that water. I ain't forgettin' that."

"Well, the water, it wasn't never ours to give. The good Lord done put it there."

The sheriff nodded. "Still, some folks might not've been so willing to share. But you listen to me, Caroline, and heed my words. This better not happen again. That boy Hammer get in trouble one more time, he goin' to jail . . . he don't end up hangin' from a tree first. That boy's wild, and I don't care how Christian you and Paul-Edward be, that boy don't straighten up, there ain't gonna be no savin' him. You understand me now?"

"I understand."

The sheriff picked up his hat from the bench and put it back on. Mama went back into the kitchen, covered a whole pan of uncut molasses bread with a clean cloth, set it in a basket, and gave it to the sheriff. The sheriff grinned on seeing that long pan of molasses bread, gave a nod of thanks to Mama, then headed back up the walkway, and Mama followed him. I left the pantry, ran through the house to a window looking out onto the side yard, and just about died when I saw who had just pulled up the driveway: Charlie, Ed-Rose, and their daddy, Old Man McCalister Simms.

Now Charlie and Ed-Rose might've been mean, but that there daddy of theirs, Old Man McCalister Simms, was rock-bottom, ornery mean. Just about everybody was scared of him and that included those children of his. It was said Old Man McCalister Simms he'd had himself two families, one by a wife near 'bout the same age as him, and after she died, a young wife, younger than his youngest daughter. Charlie and Ed-Rose were part of that second family and two of the youngest of Old Man McCalister's twelve children.

Sheriff Rankins, he saw the Simmses come up too. So did Mama. Mama stopped near the side door and didn't go out to the drive. The sheriff, he did though. He hooked the basket of molasses bread on to his saddle, then went over to the Simmses' wagon.

Old Man McCalister Simms halted the wagon and shouted, "Where's them niggers 'at done hit my Charlie?"

The sheriff spoke softly. I couldn't hear what he said. Whatever it was, it wasn't satisfying Mr McCalister Simms. He was sure enough a hard one, that Old Man McCalister Simms. "I want 'em and I wants 'em now! Ain't gonna 'low them niggers gettin' away with this!"

The sheriff, he gone on talking soft-like. Old Man McCalister Simms sat on the wagon seat frowning, looking meaner than ever. Finally he gave a nod and the sheriff stepped away from the wagon and motioned to Mama to come over. "Caroline!" he called. "You come on over here now, and you tell that boy David t' get on out here too!"

Before Mama could call me, I had the door open and was out. "Where Ma Rachel?" she asked.

"She still 'sleep," I said.

"Least that's something," Mama said, and crossed the side yard to the wagon with me by her side. Up close to Charlie now, I could see his face was all bruised up and swollen, and there was a wrapping around the top of his head. If I wasn't standing there so scared, I would've smiled with a lot of satisfaction that my brother Hammer had given Charlie the whipping that had been coming to him for so long. But there was no smiling right then; Hammer and I were in enough trouble. I didn't want any more.

"Now, Caroline," said the sheriff, "I done talked to Mr Simms and his boys, Charlie and Ed-Rose here, and he done agreed not to put your boys in jail. 'Stead, he's gonna be mighty generous with y'all and let your boys work the summer on his place, seein' your boys done half-crippled Charlie. There's a lot gotta be done Charlie would've been doin' his ownself, your boys hadn't've beaten him so. Your boys gonna hafta take up the slack."

Mama nodded.

"All right then. Startin' tomorrow, first thing!" The sheriff then turned to his horse and got ready to mount.

But then Old McCalister Simms said, "I want 'em whipped."

Mama nodded. "Yes, suh. I plans t' get on Hammer 'bout this when I see him. He won't be doin' this again. No, suh! When his papa come home, he'll wear him out."

Old Man Simms shook his head. "Naw. Naw, that ain't the way it gonna be. I want 'em whipped now."

For the first time I saw a fear in Mama's eyes. "But . . . but they papa, he ain't here."

"Then you do it," said Old Man McCalister Simms. "You a strong-lookin' gal. You welt them boys good yo'self. You don't, I will."

Mama shook her head, not saying no, just unbelieving. "Hammer . . . he ain't here."

"Then you get him. You get him back here, and you lay a strap on him and this boy too. We ain't goin' 'til you do."

The sheriff looked at Mama, then turned to the old man. "Now, look here, Mr Simms, I don't think there's no call for all this—"

"No call? Them niggers done jumped my boy, ain't they? I had my way, I'd do more'n lay a strap to 'em. I 'member the time we would've done already took these two little niggers to a tree for what they done. Can still do it!"

"Don't want that kind of talk now."

"Ain't gonna jus' be talk, I hafta wait up here much longer! One nigger get away with hittin' a white man, what you think come next? I got a good mind to deal with this my own way, me and mine. I get finished with 'em, I guarantee ya they won't be raisin' their fists again t' 'nother white man!"

The sheriff stared at him, then I s'pose he was figuring there was nothing else he could do, because he turned back to Mama and said, "Caroline, you best get Hammer and your whippin' strap, and you do what you told 'bout Hammer and David.''

"But . . . but David, he ain't done nothin'! He ain't hit that boy, Charlie Simms!"

"Now, Caroline—" started the sheriff, but then Old Man McCalister broke in.

"Ya meanin' t' stand there, gal, and tell me jus' one of your boys done this t' my Charlie?"

Mama pulled to her full height, and clasped her hands. "Yes, suh! Your boy done hit my David and ya can see he gots a bad leg here, and my Hammer done hit your boy 'cause of it!" As afraid as Mama must've been, I could still hear the pride in her voice over Hammer for standing up for me. Scared as I was, I couldn't help myself for being proud too.

Old Man McCalister Simms turned his mean ole eyes on to Charlie. "Thought you said both them boys jumped on you."

Charlie's eyes went wild. He looked at Ed-Rose, at the sheriff who was standing silent, as if not wanting to get into this. "Well . . . well, it's the truth, Daddy! She lyin'! That David, he lyin' too! It was both of 'em jumped me! I'd've been lookin' like this if they'd've fought me fair? No, suh! They jumped me—both of 'em—from behind, Pa, and they ain't give me a chance to defend myself! It's the truth, Daddy! It's the truth!"

Old Man McCalister Simms stared into Charlie, then slowly turned and looked, not at Mama, but at the sheriff, at another white man, and said, "If I thought Charlie couldn't beat one little nigger, I'd whip him myself. Had t' be both of 'em jumped him. Now what ya gonna do?"

Sheriff Peterson Rankins nodded, as if that was a certainty, that no lone little Negro could whip a near-grown white boy. After all, what would it look like if one black boy could whip a white boy who was bigger and older? "You done heard, Caroline. Now you get that Hammer, and you get that whippin' strap."

Mama bit at her lower lip. She looked down at me, and she shook her head. "No, suh. No, suh, I . . . I ain't gonna whip my David. He ain't the one done the hittin'—"

I touched her arm. "Hammer, he done what he done 'cause of me, Mama. I take my lickin' right 'long side him."

Mama's eyes looked straight into mine, and they was full. "All right then," she said. "Go on and get your brother."

I backed away, not wanting to leave Mama alone,

but I knew I had to go. She gave me a nod, letting me know she'd be all right, so I turned and would've gone for Hammer right then if it hadn't been for Ma Rachel; she was standing in the doorway. "What's that goin' on out there, Caroline?" Ma Rachel called. "What them white folks doin' on our land?"

Fast as I could, I limped back to the house trying to stop Ma Rachel before she said too much more. She was still standing in the doorway when I got to her, but her talking ain't stopped. "What's they doin'?" she asked me. "That the sheriff? That Peter Rankins standin' up there? What ya doin' here, Peter Rankins?" she hollered. "Yo' mama knows you up here? I'm gonna sho 'nough tell her—"

"Ma Rachel," I said, trying to stay quiet as I could, trying to keep Ma Rachel quiet, trying not to upset her any more. But Ma Rachel kept on ranting, kept ranting loudly too, and there I was, little ole boy on a crutch trying to keep my grandmama from cussing out these white folks and getting us into even more trouble. "Ma Rachel, come on back inside now," I pleaded. "Come on back."

"What they doin' here?" she asked me.

"They just come for water, like always," I lied. "They be gone in a minute."

"You, nigger boy!" cried Mr McCalister Simms.

"Don't you think you can get 'way! I'll see ya dead, ya try!"

I glanced back, saw the sheriff and Mama talking to Mr Simms, and hoped none of those crazy Simmses would come to the house after me.

"What they means?" cried Ma Rachel. "I heard 'em! What's they mean?"

I took Ma Rachel's arm. "You know Mr McCalister Simms, Ma Rachel. You know how he talks. He just talkin' and bein' mean and ornery like he always is."

"Well . . . I wants him off this land."

"Yes, ma'am."

"Wants 'em all off!"

"Yes'm," I said again and led her back into the house.

"Got no business here. They done took my name. They got no business here."

"Yes'm," I said one more time and wondered how I was going to go get Hammer with Ma Rachel's mind off in the last century again. Lord must've seen me struggling there in all my confusion because it was then Aunt Callie came on the back porch.

"What's goin' on in here, David?" she said soon as she was in the house and saw me holding on to Ma Rachel. "Heard hollerin'. What's goin' on?" Aunt Callie, like always, had come up to the house the back way and she hadn't seen all the commotion by the well on the other side.

Ma Rachel sat down in her rocker and stared out at the drive. Aunt Callie's gaze followed hers. "They's on our land," said Ma Rachel softly, as if that should explain everything that needed explaining. "They's on our land."

I motioned to Aunt Callie and we left Ma Rachel staring out the window and went out to the back porch. I told Aunt Callie right quick what was going on. Aunt Callie turned towards the drive.

"It's gonna be all right," I said. "Mama done worked it out with the sheriff. All Hammer and me gotta do is take a lickin'. That's all. But I gotta go get him. I gotta go get him now!"

Aunt Callie looked around nervously and nodded. "Then you go on. I take care of Ma."

I glanced through the window at Ma Rachel, still sitting where we'd left her staring out at the drive, looked at Aunt Callie once more, then took off down the porch. Fast as I could on that gimpy ole leg of mine, I crossed to the deep woods on the other side of the pasture and made my way along the cowpath, then crossed through brush and grass where there was no path at all, 'til I come to where Halton and Hammer were waiting at Papa's praying rock. It was a good place to wait. Papa prayed there every day when he was home.

I took a moment to get my breath, then I told them. I told them everything, everything about the sheriff, about the Simmses, about the whipping strap waiting for Hammer and me. I told them we had to hurry.

Hammer shook his head and sat down. "Naw. I ain't going."

"But ya gotta," I said. "It's the only way outa this thing."

"Said I ain't going."

I looked up at Halton, needing his help. Hammer could be as stubborn as an ole mule, and I knew he meant what he said.

Halton looked at me, looked at Hammer, and his sunny face took on a downward set. "Hammer, now you listen to me, boy. You think you can lay me out the way you done Charlie Simms?"

Hammer's eyes narrowed as he turned to Halton. "Why'd I wanna lay you out?"

"'Cause that's what you gonna hafta do, you don't get up from that stump and go on back to the house and get this thing over with. 'Cause you don't, I'm gonna knock you out and take you back!"

Hammer crossed his arms. "Then, Halton, you gonna hafta knock me out, 'cause I ain't going. I ain't takin' no lickin' front of the likes of Charlie Simms."

"Boy, use your head," I said. "This here's serious. I'm gonna take a lickin' too. I don't wanna, but I'm gonna take it 'cause we don't, we gonna hafta leave this place. We stay and don't take this lickin' and then go work for the Simmses, there ain't gonna be nothin' but trouble and heartache for this family. Now you figure Charlie Simms and your pride worth killin' our family for?" Hammer didn't say a word. I laid my crutch upon the ground. "Now I know you bigger'n I am and you can whip me most likely, but I'm gonna try'n whip you myself t' make you get up from there and come on back."

Hammer just sat there.

I balled up my fists. "Well?"

For the first time Hammer smiled. "Boy, pick up that crutch," he said. Then he glanced at Halton and got up. "I take this whippin', I ain't gonna cry for 'em."

Halton and I both laughed. "What you mean you ain't gonna cry, ya little scound?" asked Halton. He hooked his arm around the back of Hammer's neck. "Ya little hard-headed scound, ya never do cry!"

"Come on," I said, and got my crutch. "Let's get it over with."

When we got back to the house, Mama, the sheriff,

Old Man McCalister Simms, Charlie, and Ed-Rose were there waiting by the well. Mr Clinton Melbourne, he was there too, filling his water barrels.

"Hammer," Mama said, "go bring the strap." Hammer, he looked at Mama, eyes ain't changed, turned, and went to the barn and brought back the whipping strap. He handed it to Mama, and Mama gave him a nod. "Get them shirts off," she ordered.

We done as she said. Mama lifted the strap. It was then Ma Rachel came storming from the house. Aunt Callie was right behind trying to take hold of her. "Don't ya whip them boys, Caroline!" Ma Rachel cried. "Don't ya do it! Don't ya whip 'em!"

Mama, her voice cold as December water, turned to Aunt Callie. "Callie, you and Halton, y'all get Ma back in that house! Y'all get her back in there now. Don't let her back out here . . . and keep her 'way from them windows!"

Both Aunt Callie and Halton took hold of Ma Rachel and turned her towards the house, but Ma Rachel, she ain't stopped raving. "Lord have mercy! White folks on our land! They's makin' you whip them boys jus' like they done whipped my mama! On our own land! Don't ya do it, girl! We's free now! Don't ya do it! Ya hear me! Don't ya do it!"

Nobody said a word. Not the sheriff. Not the

Simmses. Everybody knew about Ma Rachel. Or thought they knew. Mama waited. She waited until Halton and Aunt Callie got Ma Rachel back inside, waited until the door closed, waited until Ma Rachel's screams grew faint, then she lifted the strap once more, and laid into Hammer and me.

Mama had whipped us before, but never like this. That strap tore into our legs, ripped into our backsides, cut across our backs, and Hammer and I just stood there and took it. The sheriff looked on solemnly. Old Man McCalister watched, face unchanging, mean-looking as always. Charlie and Ed-Rose watched, grinning. Mr Melbourne turned away, like he was embarrassed to be a witness to it.

Through it all, Hammer and me, we ain't protested not one bit. We just stood there taking that whipping. 'Course Hammer didn't cry. No one expected him to. Hammer never cried. But I didn't cry either. The tears came, but I didn't let them fall, not in front of the Simmses. Like Hammer, I refused to give the Simmses the satisfaction. I think that disappointed Mama. I think she wanted us to cry so she could stop whipping us, so Old Man McCalister Simms would be satisfied and tell her to stop. Finally Mama stopped on her own. "That's all," she said. "I ain't whippin' 'em no more."

THE WELL

The sheriff nodded and looked at the Simmses. Old Man Simms cut us a mean look, then got on his wagon. It was over. "Them boys, I 'spect them on my place workin' my fields come daybreak."

Mama nodded. "I'll bring 'em myself."

With that, Old Man McCalister Simms, Ed-Rose and Charlie Simms rolled away with a load of our water in their wagon. The sheriff mounted his stallion and rode away with Mama's pan of molasses bread hanging from his saddle. Mr Melbourne, without a word, left too with his own barrels of water. Mama dropped the strap, looked at Hammer and me, and ran to the house.

She was crying.

"They gonna pay for that," said Hammer, and I knew he was talking about Mama's hurt.

"You better leave it alone," I warned.

"They gonna pay."

Before I could say anything more, Aunt Callie came to the door and called for Hammer and me to come inside. "I got some salve for them welts," she said. "Best let me put it on."

Hammer and me, we were too spent to argue, so we gone on to the house and those bruises on my back, my legs, my bottom were hurting, paining so bad they slowed me way down. Hammer walked slow too. I looked at him, but he ain't looked back. Just the same, I knew he had to be hurting as bad as I was.

When we got inside the house, first voice we heard was Ma Rachel's. "She oughtn've done it!" she cried. "Caroline, she oughtn've done it."

"She ain't had no choice, Ma Rachel," I said. "Mama ain't had no choice."

"She done what she had to do," said Hammer. "We ain't holding it against her."

Ma Rachel shook her head, then slumped into her rocking chair. "They jus' takes everything. They takes everything. Come up here gettin' our water. They takes the water and don't think nothin' 'bout it, takes it and still treat us like we ain't got no feelings. Like we don't hurt none. They takes the water jus' like they done took my name."

I sat down beside Ma Rachel and listened, listened even though I had heard these words all before. "They done took my name," she said. "Wouldn't let me have it 'cause the mistress up at the plantation done had her baby 'round the same time I was born, and she wanted to call that child of hers Rachel. My mama, she done already give me my name, but the mistress, she said I couldn't keep it, said she ain't wantin' no Negroes on her place carryin' the same name as her child. My mama said they told her she better name me Pansy or Daisy or something, after some flower, and so that's what the white folks called me. Pansy. But my mama she ain't called me that. She called me Daughter front of other folks' hearin', called me Rachel when it was jus' us. Rest of my family, they called me Sister, jus' that, Sister. Mama said she better not ever hear them callin' me no Pansy, 'cause I wasn't no Pansy. My name was Rachel.

"Then there come the time the mistress she done heard my mama calling me by my name of Rachel, and she done told my mama to call me Pansy, but Mama said naw, she wasn't gonna do that 'cause my name was Rachel. So then the mistress she got mad, and she done had my mama's arms tied to a post and done whipped my mama, done whipped my mama right in front of me 'cause my mama, she ain't give up my name. And that ole mistress, she said, 'What's her name? What's her name?'

"And Mama, she said, 'Rachel.'

"And that ole she mistress she done whipped on my mama some more. 'What's her name?' she said. 'What's her name?'

"Mama said Rachel again, and that ole mistress kept on whippin' on Mama. Then she told Mama she was gonna bring me over and whip me, she don't say what my name is, and Mama . . . and Mama . . . she done give in. She done give in, 'cause she ain't wanted that ole she mistress t' be whippin' on me."

Ma Rachel, she gave a great sigh, and went on. "Well, when that ole she mistress asked her again what my name was, my mama, she done said Pansy. My mama, she done took that whippin' that day, but she ain't never give up my name. She done kept on callin' me Daughter front of other folks, but at night when she tucked me in, when nobody but me and her and God could hear, she called me Rachel, 'cause that's my name. She said don't never to forget it. That's my name—Rachel—but them white folks, they done tried t' take it from me. They done whipped my mama, but I still gots my name. Rachel! I still gots my name!"

She still had it all right. So did three of my cousins. We were passing it on.

Aunt Callie knelt in front of Ma Rachel, put her arms around her and hugged her tight. But Ma Rachel, she ain't showed a sign of knowing Aunt Callie was there; she was off in another time. Aunt Callie, she saw that and said to Hammer and me, "Y'all come on now and let me put on this salve."

Hammer and me, we were about to do as she said,

when Mama came in the room and took the salve from Aunt Callie. "Naw," Mama said. "Naw. I'm the one done whipped 'em. I'm the one done cut them welts on 'em, and I'm gonna be the one sees t' 'em healin'. I'm gonna be the one."

The next morning, long before dawn, Hammer and me, Mama and Ma Rachel, and Halton too were up. We did our morning chores, ate our breakfast, and said our morning prayer. We were going to get through this day, Mama promised us. We were going to get through every day until this thing was passed. There wasn't going to be any temper rising, she said, looking straight at Hammer. There wasn't going to be no more trouble, not over the likes of Charlie Simms. It was over, she said.

I nodded; Hammer didn't.

It wasn't fair, what we had to do, work the Simmses' field, dawn-break to dusk-set, then go home and do what work we could on our place until near midnight, sleep a little bit, then start the routine all over again. It wasn't fair, what we had to do because Hammer hit a white boy. It wasn't fair, 'cause we knew if Charlie'd just hit me, and Hammer hadn't hit him at all, none of this would've been. There would've been no sheriff calling, no whipping demanded, and certainly no work time. It wasn't fair, but that was just the way it was. That was just the way it was between black and white.

Hammer couldn't forget the humiliation of being whipped in front of Charlie and Ed-Rose and their daddy. I couldn't forget it either, but I set it aside. I figured there was something more important than a knock to Charlie Simms' face to put my life on the line for. I told that to Hammer, but he just grunted and said it wasn't over yet, this thing between him and Charlie Simms.

He was right.

Each day we worked the Simmses' place, Charlie and Ed-Rose just took a real pleasure in taunting at us, making fun, ordering us around. Like one time when George Melbourne and Dewberry Wallace had come up to the place, Charlie told Hammer and me to come chop some wood with him and Ed-Rose. When we got to the so-called chopping place, we saw a burlap sack hanging from a tree a ways off, and Charlie told Hammer to open the sack and see what was inside. Now this sack, it was stinking something fierce and whatever was inside was still alive because the bag was moving.

"Don't hafta look inside," said Hammer. "I can tell what it is from here."

"You scairt t' look inside?" asked Ed-Rose. "Thought you was s'pose t' be so tough."

"Best you look on in there," said Dewberry Wallace. "Could be you'll find yourself hanging from a tree like that yo'self one day."

"You do hang," said Charlie, "ain't gonna be no cuttin' you down. We gonna make sure you hang there 'til you rot and you stink, jus' like what's ever in that bag. Go on, boy! That's an order! Cut that sack down, open it up, and let's see what we got!"

"I take my orders from your daddy." Hammer turned to go.

"You take 'em from us or we'll see our daddy, not your mama, whip you."

"It ain't nothin', Hammer, but a sack," I said, trying to lend him some reason. "Come on, I'll go with ya."

Hammer's look stopped me. "I'll get it my ownself." He went over to the tree, unknotted the rope that held the sack, and let it fall. Then he opened the sack and looked in. He turned his face away. The white boys laughed, all except George Melbourne.

"Go on, take it out!" called Charlie.

"Yeah, go on, put your hand right on in there and take it out!" taunted Ed-Rose.

Hammer looked cold-eyed at Charlie, then looked

into the sack, and to my surprise he reached inside. He pulled out a skunk. The white boys howled with laughter, all except George Melbourne.

"Now, how'd ya like t' find that floatin' in that fine well of y'alls?" laughed Ed-Rose.

Hammer walked slowly towards them, holding the skunk by its neck. "Don't bring it over here!" cried Charlie. "Go find yo'self a place t' get rid of it."

"I already know where to get rid of it," said Hammer, and tossed the skunk right at Charlie's face. Charlie reached up to ward the skunk off, but it was right then the skunk let go a powerful stream of stink on Charlie. Dewberry Wallace and Ed-Rose standing closest to Charlie got some of it too. All three cursed, but for the moment they were too overcome with stink to do anything, so Hammer just turned and started away, with me at his side. George Melbourne started away too, headed back towards his place. "You a part of this?" asked Hammer.

George looked back at the Simmses and Dewberry Wallace. They were out of hearing range, and too caught up in their own stink, even if they could hear his words. "I ain't put that skunk in there, that what you askin'."

"But you know'd it was there."

"Look," said George, "maybe some things they do,

I wouldn't do. But don't you be puttin' me in this thing 'tween y'all and them. I can't be takin' sides with y'all."

"Yeah," said Hammer. "Yeah. Just be thinking on that next time you and your daddy come up to get some more of our water."

Hammer went on through the woods, and I followed fast as I could. I could feel George Melbourne's eyes on us.

When we got back up towards the Simmses' house, Charlie and Ed-Rose and Dewberry Wallace came running after us, but Old Mr McCalister Simms he come out and smelled their stink. "Y'all get on 'way from here and get that stink off!" he yelled before they could lay a hand on us.

"But, Pa!" cried Charlie. "Them little niggers, they—"

"I ain't wantin' t' hear it!" cried Old Man McCalister Simms. "Y'all boys can't keep a skunk's stink offa ya while two niggers can, best not come cryin' t' me! Now, y'all get that stink on 'way from here! You niggers, y'all come on t' the fields. There's work t' do!"

Old Man McCalister Simms, he turned and stomped off. Hammer and I looked at each other and we followed, and I was thinking it was kind of funny that Old Man McCalister Simms had actually saved us from getting a beating that day. But I ain't laughed. Neither did Hammer. Hammer had turned the tables on Charlie and Ed-Rose, but neither one of us took any rejoicing in it.

Next day, out of sight of Old Man McCalister Simms, Charlie and Ed-Rose and Dewberry caught up with Hammer alone and they beat him. They beat him bad. Old Man McCalister ain't said a word about it when he saw Hammer, all bloodied up. He ain't said one word. He just told Hammer to get back to work.

All that putting up with the Simmses wasn't easy to take, but I took it. My biggest trouble was trying to make sure Hammer took it. Fact of the matter, he did pretty well for a while, but then Charlie and Ed-Rose, they began to pick on Joe.

Now Joe McCalister worked at the Simmses' place most days. They ain't paid him much—they couldn't afford to pay much—but Joe, he done whatever they said. There was some talk that Joe was somehow kin to the Simmses. It was said that Old Man McCalister Simms' given name come from his mama's family name of McCalister. It was said too one of them McCalisters was Joe's granddaddy. Anyways, whatever the truth of the matter was, Joe was always up at the Simmses' and Old Man McCalister, he put up with him. Charlie and Ed-Rose, though, they was always making fun of Joe. Joe, he just thought they were being friendly.

"'Ey, Joe!" said Charlie one late afternoon. "Ya know the Reverend Jones 'specting you to open up the church for service tonight 'bout sunset."

"T'night?" questioned Joe. "Ain't nobody said nothin' 'bout no service t'night." Joe had a right to question since, after all, he was caretaker at the church. He took on that job early and he was good at it. He was proud of it too.

"Well, that's 'cause it come up on a sudden like," Charlie went on. "Seems there's a bunch of sinners done seen the light and they wants t' join the church. Reverend said he calling a special church meeting just so's he can get 'em in the House of the Lord soon's he can. He come by here earlier lookin' for ya to tell ya to get the church ready for the service, but you was out in the fields so he told us t' let you know. Now he said no need to ring the bell."

"Not ring the bell?" asked Joe, and he was sounding mighty disappointed. Joe loved ringing that bell. "Why not? I always rings the bell!"

"Well, I don't really know, Joe," said Charlie. "Maybe the reverend's 'fraid it might scare them sinners and they'll run off. Anyways, don't you fret 'bout it. You just be sure you don't ring it. You go on now, light up the church, and you wait there 'til him and them sinners and the church members show up. Said he was countin' on ya now. Can ya do it?"

"Yes, suh, Mr Charlie. Ole Joe, he'll be right there. The pastor, he know he can count on me."

"'Course he do," said Ed-Rose.

"Wait, Joe," said Hammer. "Don't you see they foolin' ya? They don't want you ringing the bell 'cause folks would come if ya did. There's no church meeting."

"You callin' me a liar?" said Charlie.

Hammer ain't said nothing and Ed-Rose demanded, "'Sides, this your business?"

"I'll make it my business," said Hammer.

"And get yo'self whipped?"

"Leave him be," said Hammer.

"Hammer," I warned, "leave it alone."

"Joe! What you doin' still standin' up here?" asked Charlie. "Don't you let these two smart-talkin' boys get you in trouble. Now you go on and tend to your business."

Joe did as he was told and we watched him go, knowing it was most likely one of Charlie's and Ed-Rose's tricks; but there was little we could do to stop it. Joe was free to go. We weren't.

We worked on, and about sunset when we were getting ready to start for home, a wagon pulled up to the Simmses' place. It was our wagon and Papa was driving. We were two happy boys, Hammer and me. We ran to Papa as fast as we could. We climbed on the wagon and hugged him just as Old Man McCalister Simms came out of his barn. Mr McCalister Simms squinted at Papa as if trying to make out who it was we were there hugging, and he hesitated as if not quite sure. After all, Papa looked like a white man. He was small built, a bantam weight, had straight brown hair, a fearsome kind of moustache, and cream-coloured skin. He was coloured, but he could pass for white. That was because Papa's daddy was a white man.

Finally Old Man McCalister, he was sure enough who it was and he gave a grunt. "Paul-Edward," he said. "Ain't know'd you was back. Heard you was s'pose t' be lumberin' 'long the Natchez Trace."

Papa gave a nod. "Just got back." He glanced over at Hammer and me. "Come to get my boys."

Old Man McCalister Simms grunted again. "They done put in they hours." Then he turned and went back into his barn. Papa headed the wagon towards home. He answered our many questions about Kevin and Mitchell and the Natchez Trace, then after a quiet had settled in, he said, "Well, I 'spect y'all must be thinking I oughta be putting a stop to this, putting a stop to you boys working over at the Simmses'."

Hammer and me, we ain't said nothing. We just waited for Papa to get on with his words.

"Thing is, I most likely couldn't put a stop to it, even if I wanted to."

"You mean to tell me," said Hammer, "you like us working for nothing for these white folks?"

"I say that?" asked Papa.

Hammer got sulky quiet.

"You got thirteen years on you, Hammer. I figure in thirteen years you ought to know me well enough to answer that for yourself. Another thing you ought to be knowing at thirteen is that you don't lay out a white boy, not down here in Mississippi, not unless you want to find yourself hanging from a tree. Folks down here don't care if you thirteen or thirty, you do something they don't like, they'll hang a black boy soon's they will a black man 'cause they don't see no difference. It's past the time you learned that, Hammer. You too, David. Working for the Simmses might hurt your pride, mine too, but we can put up with that. Better your hurt pride than your life over the likes of Charlie Simms. You boys better start learning how to use your heads, not your fists, when it comes to white folks. You learn to out-smart them, 'cause in the end you can't out-fight them, not with your fists. They got the power, but we got our heads. Y'all understand what I'm saying?"

Well, I could see it. I didn't like it, but I could see it, and I said so. Hammer, he ain't said nothing.

Papa gave him a look and waited, I s'pose for Hammer to speak, but course Hammer just sat there, not saying a word. Then Papa said, "Y'all know my daddy was a white man. My sister and me, we were born slaves to him. That's right, he owned us, just like you'd own a dog. We were slaves because our mama was a slave, and he owned her. Now I ain't saying he ain't loved us, because I believe he did. I was just a baby when the war come that was supposed to set us free, but there wasn't no difference between the way my papa treated us before and after. He set up a house for us, and he come and spent time with us most every day, and everybody knew we was his coloured family. He seen to it that my sister and me, we got book learning, got right smart-looking clothing, got whatever he figured we needed.

"'Course now, for all that caring he done, he ain't never let me forget I was a coloured boy. There come a time he whipped me into not forgetting it. That was when his boy by his white wife up and hit me and I hit him back, knocked him down. Well, that white boy went and told our daddy, and my daddy come got me and whipped me right in front of that white son of his. I mean he laid into me good with his whipping strap. Said I had to learn that no matter how white I looked, I was still a Negro and a Negro couldn't go around hitting white folks. Said that whipping was for my own good. Said that I'd better start learning how to use my head, not my fists, if I was going to survive in this white man's world.

"Now it may sound strange to you, but I'm glad my papa whipped me that day, 'cause it made me come to a realization about myself. I might've been a white man's son, but that didn't make me white, so I took his advice. I got to be fourteen and I ran off from home, from his place, but I took his advice. I started using my head, 'stead of my fists. I got this land with my head, not my fists. My papa gave me some good advice. I think y'all best be taking it too."

Papa, he didn't say nothing more. Hammer and me, we didn't say nothing either, but I was thinking hard on what Papa had said. I was hoping Hammer was too. If he was, he wasn't giving any indication of it when he spoke up again. "Papa," he said, "you mind if we turn this wagon around and go over to the church?"

"The church? What for?" asked Papa.

We told him what Charlie and Ed-Rose had told Joe.

"We don't figure there to be a meeting," said Hammer.

"We figure they're just funnin' with Joe," I said.

"All right," Papa said, and he turned the wagon back towards the church road. Long before we reached the church, we saw the lantern lights. Joe had lit them all, and we could see them shining as we made our way through the forest. As we drew nearer to the church, we could hear Joe singing, his voice ringing loud and clear. Then we saw Charlie and Ed-Rose and Dewberry Wallace. All three were peeking into a church window and sniggering. They turned when they heard the wagon.

"What y'all doin' here?" asked Charlie as we got close. Surprise was all 'cross his face.

"Didn't expect us to show up, didja now?" asked Hammer.

Papa gave Hammer a shut-your-mouth look and stepped down from the wagon. Hammer and I got down too. "We come up to the church for a meeting," said Papa.

"There ain't no meeting," sneered Charlie. "Jus' that addle-brained fool in there holding a sermon."

"Then I s'pose the other folks must've forgot," said Papa. "Best we get on in, boys," he said to us. "We already late."

Charlie, Ed-Rose, and Dewberry stared at us in pale silence. Papa had taken the fun out of the joke on Joe. As Papa opened the door to the church, they turned and walked away.

"Y'all late!" exclaimed Joe as soon as we entered. He was standing at the altar, the big Bible on top of it, opened, even though he couldn't read.

Papa took off his hat. "I 'spect we are," he said.

"I been waitin' and waitin' for folks to come, but they ain't come so I done said the prayer and give the sermon my ownself! Jus' now done sung the hymn." He frowned. "Don't 'spect, though, I can dismiss 'til after all the folks and the reverend come."

Papa, hat in hand, walked up the aisle towards Joe. Hammer and I followed. "Don't think you have to worry 'bout that, Joe," Papa said. "Seems the reverend called off the meeting."

Joe looked surprised. "You sure, Mr Paul-Edward?"

Papa nodded. "I'm sure."

Joe continued to frown, then his face brightened. "Then I 'spect we can dismiss!"

"I 'spect so," Papa said. He stepped into a pew.

Hammer and I stepped beside him. "You got a closing song?"

"Yes, suh!" said Joe. "'Nearer My God to Thee'!" He hesitated. "That be all right?"

Papa nodded. "That'll be just fine. It's a fine song."

Joe smiled with satisfaction and began to sing. Papa, Hammer and I joined in. We sang the song in full, then Joe said the benediction, dismissed his small congregation, and we all headed for home. Joe's home was a short ways from the church, heading north. We headed south. Joe walked; we got back on the wagon. On our way home Papa took a side road to the reverend's house. It was late, the house was dark, but Papa woke the reverend up anyway and told him about Joe and the Simmses. The reverend and Papa, they agreed that the meeting the Simmses had told Joe about was cancelled. They agreed that's what they would tell Joe.

That next morning it was Papa, not Mama, who took us in the wagon up to the Simmses'. Old Man McCalister Simms saw Papa and ain't said a word. Papa ain't said a word either. "You boys mind yourselves," Papa said to us. "I'll be back come sunset." Then he turned the wagon around and headed back to our land.

And that's the way it was for the months we

worked at the Simmses' place. Every day Papa took us over there. Every day Papa came at sunset and took us home. We put in our months, and Papa and Kevin and Mitchell stayed at home and saw us through it. But we all knew that one day they would have to go back to lumbering again, and that's what they did. When our working days at the Simmses' ended, when we were finally free to spend the days on our own land, Papa and my brothers Mitchell and Kevin, they all headed back to the Natchez Trace. One week after they were gone, Hammer made a point of going back to the Simmses' farm, found Charlie alone, and knocked him down.

Again.

I was with him and not wanting to be. "Now tell that to your daddy," he said. "Tell him Hammer Logan done knocked you down . . . again! Tell him I used my fists, nothing else! Tell him that and even if he do come after me, see if you don't get your ownself whipped this time!" He said that and left Charlie sitting on the ground staring after him. Charlie didn't move to get up, but he cursed Hammer.

"Y'all gonna pay!" he yelled after us. "Y'all gonna sure 'nough pay for this!"

I knew it still wasn't over.

I braced myself and waited for the sheriff or Old Man McCalister to come calling, this time with a rope. But the days and the nights passed, and nobody came except folks wanting more water. After a while I began to think maybe nobody was coming, that maybe Charlie had decided it was best to keep what Hammer had done to himself. Two or three days after I came on that way of thinking, Mr Melbourne and George came knocking on the door. The dawn had just broke and Halton had already gone off to the fields. Ma Rachel was gone too; she had spent the night at Aunt Callie's.

"Come to get some more water, that be all right with y'all," said Mr Melbourne.

Mama stood in the doorway and talked to him. "Help yo'self," she said. "You knows you welcome to it."

"Well, I'm right obliged," Mr Melbourne said. "Thought we would've done had more rain by now and we wouldn't hafta be troublin' y'all."

"Ain't no trouble," said Mama. "No trouble at all."

"Well, I thank ya. We ain't had much of a garden, but my missus done sent ya some pickled onions and tomatoes and such, jus' to show our appreciation. Got 'em in my wagon."

"Well, ya know that ain't necessary, Mr

Melbourne, but I sure do thank ya. Thank your wife for me too. David, you go on to the wagon and get them preserves, and Hammer, you give Mr Melbourne a hand with that water."

Hammer and me, we did as we were told, and walked out with the Melbournes. Together, Hammer and George Melbourne lifted one of the empty barrels from the wagon, and Mr Melbourne took down the other. Mr Melbourne pointed out the basket his wife had sent, then he headed for the well, just as two more wagons pulled up the drive. Mr Jonas Peabody from up the road and three of his redheaded boys were on the first wagon; Mr Tom Bee with John Henry Berry beside him was on the other. Mr Melbourne set his barrel down beside the well and gave a wave. "Look like I done beat y'all to this sweet water this morning!"

Mr Peabody laughed and got down, followed by his boys. "Well, jus' don't get it all! We got us a mighty thirst!"

The Peabodys went over and stood by the well. Mr Tom Bee got down along with John Henry, and the two of them gave the Peabodys and the Melbournes a polite nod, then grinned at Hammer and me. "How y'all boys doin'?" asked Mr Tom Bee. "And how's the rest of the family?"

"Fine," we said.

"Good. Think I'll go on in and speak while's I wait my turn."

Mr Tom Bee started across the lawn.

I followed after him, carrying the basket of pickled onions and tomatoes and such. John Henry stayed with Hammer.

Hammer lifted the top off the well.

I stopped and turned. So did Mr Tom Bee.

"Lord have mercy!" exclaimed Mr Melbourne, and he stepped back from the well. Everybody standing there did the same. All hands went to their faces. "What in God's name is that stench?" cried Mr Melbourne.

I set down the basket and hurried over. Mr Tom Bee followed.

"Mama!" called Hammer, stepping back to the well. "Mama!"

Mama immediately appeared in the doorway. "What is it? What . . . what's that I smell?"

"It's the well, Mama!" I yelled to her. "It's the well!"

Mama left the doorway and ran to the well. She peered down it, down into the blackness of it. Then she unhooked the bucket from its post and lowered it, down, down into the well.

"Here, Miz Caroline, let me do that," said Mr Tom Bee.

Mama shook her head, not even turning to him. Her eyes were on the blackness of the well.

We all heard the bucket drop. We all heard the bucket fill. Then Mama pulled on the rope and began to haul water. Hammer went over to her. "Let me, Mama," he said. But again she shook her head, almost as if she didn't hear.

Hand over fist, hand over fist, she drew the water up.

The stench became almost unbearable.

The bucket was up.

Mama wrapped the rope back to its pole and peered into the water; then she shook her head. Strands of long hair lay on top of the bloody water. "Something's dead down there," she said in a voice unbelieving. "Some animal done fell in, tryin' t' get to the water." She shook her head again and moaned, "Oh, Lord . . ."

"Charlie."

Everyone's eyes settled on Hammer.

"Charlie Simms. Son-of-a—"

"Hammer!" cried Mama, not stupefied enough to let Hammer swear.

"No animal jus' done fell down there, Mama. The

top was on," Hammer said. "But some animal I know done put something foul down in there!"

"Boy, you know what you sayin'?" demanded Mr Peabody.

Mr Tom Bee stepped forward. "Now, Hammer, wait—"

"Yeah, I know."

There was only silence. A dead silence.

Mama stepped back from the well. "The Lord giveth and the Lord taketh away."

"Lord ain't had nothin' t' do with this!" exclaimed Hammer. "It was them Simmses! David knows it! They ain't never liked the fact we had water on our land and they ain't, and they had to come up here and get water. Charlie and Ed-Rose much as told David and me they'd come up and poison this well one day. They said it a time we was all down at the creek watering our cows. Another time too. Said maybe one day we'd find something dead down our well. Ain't that right, David? Ain't that what they said?"

John Henry had heard the same but Hammer didn't put his name in it, and I think John Henry was just as glad he didn't. I looked around the circle of folks, at Hammer, and nodded. "It's the truth all right."

Mr Peabody stepped forward. "Y'all know what

y'all sayin'? Y'all makin' some serious charges here."

"We know what we know," said Hammer.

I nodded again, "It's the truth."

"'Sides that," said Hammer, and looked straight at George Melbourne, "we ain't the only ones heard them say it."

John Henry looked a bit uneasy, but Hammer didn't even glance his way.

"Who else then?" asked Mr Melbourne.

"Ask your son," said Hammer.

Mr Melbourne, looking kind of puzzled now, turned to George. "You know somethin' 'bout this?"

George looked at Hammer and me, then back at his daddy. "No, suh. I was down by the creek one day they was there, and Charlie and Ed-Rose and Dewberry was there too, but I ain't heard nothin'. I can't say they done said it." He glanced again at Hammer and me, lowered his eyes, and looked away.

Mr Peabody shook his head. "Well, I can't believe it. I can't believe nobody'd be that low-down."

Mr Melbourne looked at Mama, at Hammer and me, then he said, "One way we can find out. We can ask them."

Mr Peabody looked doubtful. Mr Tom Bee was silent, letting the white men do the talking, but he looked doubtful too.

"I'll go myself," said Mr Melbourne. "I'll talk to both them boys and Old Man McCalister."

"Don't think that's gonna be necessary," said Mr Peabody as another wagon came up the road. "Look yonder."

We all looked. Old Man McCalister Simms, Ed-Rose, and Charlie were in the wagon, headed for our drive, and our well. All of us knew it without a word being spoken. Two water barrels set in the back of the wagon.

There was only silence as the wagon turned up the drive. There was only silence as the wagon came to a halt behind Mr Tom Bee's wagon. There was only silence as Old Man McCalister Simms gave a nod in greeting, and he and Ed-Rose and Charlie got down. They came over to the well.

"My, Lord! What's that I smell?" asked Mr Simms.

"Ask your boys," said Hammer, much too quickly for a little Negro boy standing there dealing with white men. "They the ones done put the stink there."

"What you talkin' 'bout, nigger?" cried Charlie.

Old Man McCalister's lined and weathered face looked to line and weather some more. "Gal!" he said, looking straight at Mama, "you best hush up that little nigger of your'n 'fore I hafta come over there and hush him up for ya!"

Mama cast a look on Hammer warning him not to speak another word; then she stepped right side of him, took hold of him, and her tall frame suddenly seemed taller. "Somebody done put something rotten and dead down our well, Mr Simms. My—my boys believe your boys the ones done it. They believes that and . . . and I gots t' know. Them boys of your'n . . . them boys, Charlie and Ed-Rose, would they go and do somethin' like that t' this sweet water? Would they now?"

Old Man McCalister's eyes turned to slits. His breathing grew heavy. He took a step forward. "I'll cut yo' heart out for what you sayin', gal!"

"You try," said Hammer and pulled from Mama's grip. "You try, and I'll see ya dead."

His words were quietly spoken and they were chilling, even to me.

Old Man McCalister Simms came no farther.

"Look here, Mr Simms," said Mr Melbourne, before Old Man McCalister took it upon himself to knock Hammer down for what he'd said, "we don't want things gettin' outa hand here. But the truth of the matter is that the only sweet water well around here been poisoned. Now you know well as I do what that mean t' everybody 'round who been usin' this well. Now I know for a fact, my brother and his boys was up here late evenin' yesterday, and they done draw'd good water. I come up first thing this mornin' t' get my family some water and this well here stinkin' like hell. Now them boys yonder—that Hammer and that David—they done said your boys, Charlie and Ed-Rose there, they done threatened t' poison this here well. Now, I wants t' know what's the truth of it!"

Mr Simms cursed and spat the ground. Mr Melbourne put up his hand, as if to stop any more such action . . . or something worse. "Now I ain't sayin' I'm takin' these boys' words on what happened. All I know is this well here done saved me and mine for some months now, and these folks here they ain't had t' share, but they done it without askin' nothin' from nobody. Now all of a sudden they water ain't no good no more, and I gotta ask why. I gotta ask why!"

"Maybe they done put something down it they ownselves," said Ed-Rose before his father could speak. "Put it down there and then now tryin' t' blame it on us!"

"Now why would we go and do a fool thing like that?" asked Hammer.

"Hush!" said Mama, but too late. The words were already spoken, and Charlie took them up.

"'Cause you figurin' you and that David could get Ed-Rose and me back for all that work y'all had t' do after jumpin on me. You figurin' t' lay the blame for a bad well on Ed-Rose and me, get everybody all riled up 'gainst us. Well, it ain't gonna work, you little nigger. Ain't nobody gonna believe yo' word over a white man's!"

"I s'pose not," said Hammer, and looked at George Melbourne. George Melbourne reddened and kept his silence. John Henry and me, our eyes met.

It was then that Joe McCalister came walking up the road. "Mornin'!" he said before he had even gotten up the drive.

Nobody said a word, but things like that didn't bother Joe. I doubt if he even noticed, because he turned his attention to the next thing on his mind.

"Mr Charlie, Mr Ed-Rose! How'd that hunt come out the other night? Bet them possums and them coons y'all done bagged was mighty good eatin'!"

Old Man McCalister Simms turned cold eyes on his boys. "Y'all gone huntin'?"

Ed-Rose and Charlie looked at each other, and all of us standing there could see their fear. "No, suh, Pa!" Ed-Rose yelped out. "We ain't!"

"Yeah, ya did," said Joe, just as friendly as always. He had no idea of what was going on. "You done forgot, huh? I seen ya."

"When y'all gone?" demanded Old Man Mc-Calister Simms. "Y'all ain't brought no hunt home for your mama t' cook in a spell now."

"Ah, Pa, ya know Joe," said Charlie. "Ya know he ain't right in the head. He makin' it up."

"Naw, I ain't!" Joe cried, getting a bit vexed about anybody doubting his word. "I done seen y'all down 'long the Rosa Lee jus' night 'fore last and I said, ''Ey, there, Mr Charlie! Mr Ed-Rose!' Y'all had done already bagged y'allselves a possum and a coon too! And I done asked y'all what y'all was gonna do with that skunk y'all done caught, and y'all done said it was for a joke and not t' tell nobody! Don't y'all 'member!"

Charlie took a step backwards. "Ah, Daddy, Joe, he jus' mad 'cause we been funnin' him. We done played a trick on him while back and he jus' mad. Daddy . . . Daddy, he lyin'—"

"Naw. Naw, he ain't," said Mr McCalister Simms. "He ain't got the brains t' lie."

"Well . . . well, then he jus' done got the days mixed up."

"That's right, Pa," said Ed-Rose. "He jus' done got

the days mixed up. He must be talkin' 'bout that last coon hunt we gone on—"

"Yeah, that's right, Pa! That's right, and that was more'n a month ago!"

Old Man McCalister stared dead-eyed at those boys of his, and he shook his head. "Naw. Naw, that ain't what happened. Y'all boys lyin' t' me."

"Naw, Pa, naw—"

"Y'all done poisoned that well."

"Ah, naw—"

"Y'all done shamed me and mine."

"No, suh, Pa!" cried Charlie. "No, suh, we ain't done no such thing. No, suh!"

"Don't you go lyin' t' me, boy!" said Mr McCalister Simms and with one mighty fist knocked Charlie to the ground. "It's one thing t' teach a nigger where he stand, but ya don't go destroyin' God's good earth t' do it!" He reached inside his wagon. He pulled out a bullwhip.

Charlie's eyes and Ed-Rose's too got bigger. "Naw, Pa!" yelled Ed-Rose, backing away.

"Pa! Pa! Don't ya do it!" cried Charlie from the ground. "Don't ya go shamin' us like this front of niggers!"

"Y'all done already shamed yo'selves!" shouted the old man. "Get up!"

THE WELL

"Please, Pa! Please!" Charlie cried again as he got
up. "Not front of niggers!"

Old Man McCalister Simms stood there breathing
hard and trembling with his rage; then he stepped
back. "Charlie, you and Ed-Rose, y'all get down in
that well and get them dead things outa there!"

"But, Pa—"

Mr McCalister Simms cracked the whip upon the
ground. "Don't y'all back talk me! There was only
white men standin' up here, y'all wouldn't be talkin'
at all! Now, y'all done put that filth down there, y'all
get it out, and don't y'all stop 'til it's all out! Y'all
hear me? Not 'til it's all out! Charlie, you the one go
down first!"

Ed-Rose and Charlie backed away from their
daddy, looked at the Peabodys and the Melbournes,
but not at Mr Tom Bee, John Henry, Hammer, Mama,
or me. I reckon they were too shamed to look at us.
They got a rope from their wagon, and Ed-Rose lowered Charlie down into the well. It took them a while,
and we all waited. Charlie came up wet and shivering
without a thing, and Mr McCalister Simms sent Ed-
Rose down. We waited some more. Back and forth
the brothers went, taking turns going down. They
brought up parts of a possum, a coon, and a skunk
too, and went back down. Seeing those parts, all of

us standing there knew Ed-Rose and Charlie hadn't taken any chances about spoiling our well. They hadn't just thrown dead animals down there in the night; they'd hacked them up before they did.

The time passed and more folks, coloured folks and white folks, their wagons filled with empty barrels, came up the road, and there was a buzz of words softly passed about what the Simmses had done, and a silence settled over the wagons, and the day.

Finally it was Charlie who brought the last of the dead things out. "Y'all got it all?" Old Man Mc-Calister demanded of Charlie.

Charlie, eyes lowered, nodded. "All we can, Daddy."

"Then y'all get on in that wagon . . . in the back!"

Charlie placed the last dead thing in the back of their wagon, and he and Ed-Rose got in with them. Mr McCalister Simms climbed on the seat, took up the reins, and turned the mules down the drive. As the Simmses passed all those wagons lined up for water, all those silent, accusing eyes, Charlie and Ed-Rose hung their heads. Old Man McCalister, though, stared dead-eyed, straight ahead.

Folks watched the wagon until it was gone, out of sight, then the folks began to leave. Mr Melbourne and George left, and the Peabodys too. All the folks left, all with empty barrels.

The possum and the coon and the skunk—most parts of them anyway—were out of the well, but the water was spoiled just the same. All the good well water was gone now, and everybody suffered because of what Charlie and Ed-Rose had done. Eventually, though, the well was drained, the earth cleaned itself out, and the water was good again. In a few years another dry spell came, and again everybody's well went dry. Everybody's except ours. Folks came again to draw the water, and Mama and Papa shared it as freely as before. Coloured folks, and white folks too, came for that sweet water. Everybody came, everybody except the Simmses. As long as Old Man Mr McCalister Simms lived, we never saw any of the Simmses set foot on our land again.